" "

CONVERSATIONS IN JUNE

Richard Anderson

Conversations in June

Copyright © 2016 Richard Anderson

All Rights Reserved.

Printed by www.lulu.com

ISBN 978-1-326-58564-8

CONTENTS

THE FIRST YEAR
    June 21st 11
    June 25th 30

THE SECOND YEAR
    June 2nd 41

THE HOLIDAY
    September 19th 70
    October 6th 95

" "

CONVERSATIONS IN JUNE

Richard Anderson

Life is never fair, and perhaps it is a good thing for most of us that it is not

— Oscar Wilde

CONVERSATIONS IN JUNE

" "

CONVERSATIONS IN JUNE

THE FIRST YEAR
JUNE 21st

Robin and Jordan were on the patio when I got to the house. It was hot and the June sun was high and white. Jordan had his feet up on a big wooden table. He was wearing a pair of green shorts and nothing else. My sister was in her black and white bikini. Her dark blonde hair was tied behind her head so you could see all the freckles on her shoulders.

'Here he is,' Jordan said as I stepped up to the patio.

Robin stood up. 'Hey Will,' she said, smiling. We hugged. She offered me a drink and sat down.

'I can't,' I said. 'I'm driving.'

'One won't hurt you,' Jordan said.

'Maybe it will. I drink too much as it is.'

'Sit down,' Robin said. 'Relax.'

I sat down. 'How are you both?' I asked.

'We're fine,' Jordan said. 'How about you? Where's your girl?'

'I'm fine,' I said. 'Sophia's busy today.' I looked around. 'Where's Abigail?'

'She's hiding.'

'Hiding?'

'We told her you were coming so she's hiding,' Robin said. 'You should find her. You two haven't played hide and seek in a long time.'

I looked behind the big palm trees next to the house. I thought I could see her kneeling in the shade beside a bush. How do trees grow so close to the sand? I wondered.

'She's a devil,' Jordan said. 'She's bloody good at hiding because she cheats. And she's quiet. You never really know where she is.'

'Quit saying *bloody*,' Robin said.

'Come on then. Where is she?' I said.

'We're not telling you,' Robin said. 'Find her yourself. When did you become so grouchy?'

'I'm not grouchy,' I argued. 'Just hot.'

'Take off your sweater and have a drink.'

Jordan lit a cigarette and poured a small glass of whiskey. I took off my sweater. I could feel the cool air going up the short sleeves of my T-shirt.

Just then Abigail came running up to the patio from the trees. Her hair was loose and wavy.

CONVERSATIONS IN JUNE

'Ah,' I said, smiling. 'There you are.'

'Gave up in the end, did you?' Jordan said to her disappointedly.

Abigail went to Robin.

'You look uneasy, Will,' Jordan said. 'Have a drink. Relax.'

'I'm alright thanks.'

'How long will you stay?' Robin asked me.

'I'm not sure,' I said.

Robin looked at Abby. 'You remember your Uncle Will, don't you?'

Abby nodded shyly. She was looking at me with her bright blue eyes. 'I've missed you,' I said to her. She came over to me and we hugged. 'Her hair has grown,' I said to Robin. 'Last time I saw her it was short. She looked like a little Marilyn Monroe.' I looked at Abigail. 'You'll grow up looking like your mum. You have freckles just like her.'

'I hate my freckles but they're lovely on Abby,' Robin said.

'There's nothing wrong with freckles,' I said.

'I count them when I can't sleep,' Jordan said. He crossed his arms. 'She adds more every week.'

'She probably does,' I said.

'Stop being silly,' Robin said.

'I'm not being silly,' Jordan grinned. 'I think you're the most beautiful woman in the world.'

'Now you're really being silly.'

Jordan pinched her leg.

'Stop it.' She slapped him and he fell back, smiling. 'Not while Will is here.'

'Oh, I don't care,' I lied.

'Lighten up you two,' Jordan laughed. 'Will's seen it all before, haven't you?' He looked at me carefully. His eyes narrowed. 'How is that girl of yours anyway?'

'She's fine,' I said. Jordan pouted and looked away. I had a feeling that I had derailed the conversation.

'What shall we talk about to pass the time?' Jordan asked. He was twirling his thumbs.

'How's the book going?' Robin asked me.

'Very well,' I said.

'I'd like to read it when you're done. How much have you got left to do?'

'About fifty pages,' I said.

'Oh. That's not so bad. You should have it done by the end of the summer.'

'I hope so.'

'Are you going to publish it?' Jordan asked.

'Sure.'

Jordan lit another cigarette.

'Writing makes me feel great,' I said. 'It's one of the best things in the world.'

CONVERSATIONS IN JUNE

'I think you should take a break from it,' Jordan said. 'You're at it all the time. I don't know where you get the patience. I couldn't sit at a desk all day and write like you do. That sort of thing would bore me.'

'And you don't even read,' Robin put in.

'Nope. I don't read. I don't write. I'm a sportsman and you know it. I love my football. Abby loves football too, don't you?'

Abigail nodded. Robin ran her hands through her hair. I could see her henna tattoo snaking up her left arm.

Jordan was grinning. 'Abigail's not very good at it but she still loves to play.'

Robin slapped him. 'Of course she's good at it. Don't say things like that to her. You know what she's like. She'll believe you. Our daughter will grow up thinking she's no good at anything.'

'I like throwing but I don't like catching,' Abby said. I smiled when she said this. It was nice to hear her talk.

'Of course you can catch,' Robin said.

'It's alright Abby,' I said. 'I'm no good at catching or throwing, even at my old age.'

'You're not old, Will,' Jordan said. 'I don't understand half the crap you say.'

'I was joking,' I said.

Jordan smirked. For a while we stopped talking. I could hear the sound of the surf and the trees rustling in the light breeze.

'Hey, Will,' Jordan muttered.

'What?'

'Just back to the book thing… why don't you write something intelligent? Why don't you write something that's beneficial to the world?'

I lifted my head. 'Like what?'

'Like an encyclopaedia or something like that. Yeah. That's it. You should write a brand new encyclopaedia – one to end them all.'

'That's ridiculous. Do you have any idea how much time that would take and how much studying I would have to do?'

Jordan shrugged. He didn't know at all. He was just drunk. 'Then write something people can relate to. Write something that'll change the world. Write something that'll change the universe.'

'That's impossible,' I said.

'Why the hell is it?'

'Because it's impossible to change the universe through writing. You can change the world, sure. But you can't change the universe. That's too much.'

Jordan was getting excited. 'Then change the world if you can't change the universe,' he said. 'Write something new. Something fresh. Print a

CONVERSATIONS IN JUNE

thousand copies and pass them to random people in the street. Make posters and business cards you can slip into your wallet. Go mail copies through letterboxes up and down the country. Go record an audio book.' He sniffed. 'Take the world by storm, Will. You could be writing about, well, I don't know. That's for you to decide. Are you listening to me? Do you understand?'

'Yes, Jordan, I am listening to you and I do understand, but I think you might have had too much to drink. I don't care about changing the world.'

Jordan leaned forward. 'Listen to what I have to say about writing, Will. Just hear me out now.' He cleared his throat. 'To me, Will, writing is like playing football. When you play you play to win. You put everything on the table. When I play football I get into a zone. I play like a champion, and nothing else matters except the ball, the team, and winning. And I mean *truly* winning. I aim to win every time I play no matter what gets in my way. I put everything out there every time. I throw everything in, Will. I hope you understand.' He paused to take a drink. 'What I'm saying, Will, is that writing is the same. You've got to put everything in. You sit at a desk and write a story the way I run onto a pitch and play football. We are artists. We must perform with all the grace God has given to us. That's the way I see things. I play as hard as I can, and most of the time it pays off. You've got to play hard too. You've got to write like a champion and win.'

'Oh quite jabbering,' Robin said. 'I've heard enough. You've had way too much to drink.'

'Whatever,' Jordan huffed. 'I know what I'm trying to say. And I don't care how much I've had to drink. I feel good. Really good. Really, really good. I feel like I could go out there right now and play the greatest game of my life with only half my team – and I'd win, too, in true godlike fashion. Do you ever get like that, Will? Do you ever feel like a god when you're writing?'

'I think so. I'm sure all writers and artists have their moments.'

'When I'm hyped to play football I play like a professional. When you're hyped to write a story I bet you write like a professional.'

'I'll have a drink,' I said.

'Good man. Welcome to the fold.'

'I've been chewing it over for a while.'

'I think Jordan's definitely had too much,' Robin said.

'Whatever. You're just jealous of my superior sporting capabilities.'

'Enough now,' Robin said. 'I won't have you making a scene in front of our daughter.'

CONVERSATIONS IN JUNE

'Fine.' Jordan fell back and took a drink. He put his head against the back of the chair and closed his eyes. 'One of these days we'll play football, Will. Then I'll show you what I mean. I'll show you what makes a true sportsman.'

In fifteen minutes he was fast asleep.

'Are you alright?' I asked Robin.

'Yeah,' she said. 'I'm okay.'

'Happy?'

'Happy.'

'What a word to pin down,' I said.

'What do you mean?'

'Happy,' I repeated.

'Don't go all funny on me, Will.'

'I was just thinking about it. It's so quiet out here that every word you speak seems heavier somehow.'

'I don't want to talk like this,' Robin said.

'Okay. How do you want to talk?'

'I want to talk about happy things.'

'Like what?' I said.

'Happy things,' Robin said.

'Aren't you happy?' I asked.

'I am happy.'

'Honestly?'

'Yes, Will, I'm happy. Now can you please stop asking me?'

'Is Jordan here giving you trouble?'
'No.'
'Robin.'
'What?'
'Is he giving you trouble?'
'No.'
'Promise?'
'I promise,' Robin said. 'I'm sorry. I know you're concerned about me.'
'I'm sorry too,' I said.
'What for?'
'For not coming to visit sooner.'
'Better now than never,' Robin shrugged.
'Yeah, I suppose so. But I should've come earlier. I haven't been a great brother lately.'
'Have you been busy?' Robin asked.
'A little, yeah,' I said.
'How's work?'
'Same as ever. How about you?'
'Same as ever, yeah,' Robin said.
'Time goes much faster these days,' I said.
'Why do you think that?'
'I don't know really.'
'Maybe you're too busy.'
'Probably. It's confusing.'
'Are you happy?' Robin asked. 'Come on. You can tell me. I'd like it if you told me.'

CONVERSATIONS IN JUNE

'To be honest with you, Robin, I am happy. I haven't been this happy in a very long time.'

'Are you being honest with me? Really? Usually when people say they're being honest or frank it means they're really not.'

'I am being honest with you. Honest to God.'

'Come on now,' Robin said. She tilted her head. 'Tell me the truth.'

'Yes. Really. I am very happy. My writing is going well. Sophia is happy. My friends are okay. You're all happy.' I nodded. 'I'm happy.'

'Do you still get lonely?'

'Sometimes,' I said.

'Is that why you're here?' Robin asked.

'No. I came here because I missed you.'

'Are you lonely at the moment, Will?'

'A little,' I said. 'It comes and goes.'

'You should tell me these things.'

'I'm afraid to tell you.'

'Why?' Robin asked.

'I'm afraid I'll get in your way. You have a family to maintain after all.'

'You're family too, Will.'

'Yeah,' I said. 'I know. So how about you? Do you still get lonely?'

'Yes. I do. I miss Mum and Dad. All the time.'

'I miss them too.'

I lowered my head.

'I could do with them sometimes,' Robin said.

'Yeah. Me too.'

'It's difficult. Sometimes too difficult.'

I looked at her. 'Don't get upset,' I said.

'I'm not.'

'I know when you're upset.'

'Sorry,' Robin said.

'Don't be sorry,' I looked out at the beach. 'Abigail's wandered off,' I said.

'She'll be okay. Trust me. She knows her limits. She's smart. As long as I can see her.'

We stopped talking for a minute.

'Jordan doesn't give you grief, does he?' I asked, staring at the sea.

'No.'

'I know when you're lying to me,' I said.

Robin said nothing.

'Come on,' I said. 'Talk to me. You can talk to me about anything. Anything and everything.'

'Well... Jordan's drinking habits are getting a lot worse. He used to drink twice a week. Now he's drinking almost every day and every time he does he gets drunk. He doesn't do anything to me though. He just goes up to bed. Or he'll come out here and play football on his own. He pretends to be a superstar. It's pretty funny.'

CONVERSATIONS IN JUNE

'You ought to keep an eye on him,' I said.

'He'd never hurt me. He's afraid of me. I heard him say it once. But I'm not sure he was serious. I get scared sometimes when he's around.'

'Do you ever feel trapped?' I asked.

'God no. I have the beach to come down to.'

'Not in the winter,' I said.

'Oh no. I walk down here all the time in the winter. I just wrap up in coats. But I'm never out for long because I hate leaving Abigail alone with him. I hate it. I've always hated it.' She was playing with her hands. 'I don't know. I just don't like leaving her with him for longer than fifteen minutes.'

'I'm sure he's fine with her. And you're a mother after all. Of course you hate leaving her.'

'I don't think I trust him. Subconsciously I mean. Or something like that. I don't know.' She put her hand on her forehead. 'I love my daughter more than Jordan anyway. I'd do anything for her, Will. Anything at all. Dad always doubted me. He used to say I'd be a lazy mother.'

'No way,' I said. 'You're a great mother.'

'Thanks.'

'Dad loved you, Robin. I'm sure he didn't mean any of the bad things he used to say.' I rubbed her arm. 'Now come on. Let's lighten up. How about we play some football?'

I got up. Suddenly I was full of energy.

'Yeah, alright. It might help,' Robin said.

'You know it will.'

~

That night while Jordan and Abby were asleep in the house we took a walk down to the beach to see the glowing surf. 'The surf glows blue in the summertime but only for a week,' Robin said to me as we walked barefoot down the narrow, sand-covered path to the beach. The night air was cool and the sand between my toes was cold and dry.

'I thought you didn't like leaving Abigail for longer than quarter of an hour,' I said.

'How long has it been?'

'About thirty minutes.'

'I'm just comfortable I guess,' Robin said. 'And he's asleep anyway. He sleeps well after beer.'

'Do I help?'

'Of course you do.'

I put my hand on her shoulder.

'How do you feel?' I asked.

'I feel pretty fine. How do you feel?'

'I feel fine too,' I said. 'I don't feel sad. I don't feel stressed. I don't feel alone. I feel good.'

'Good.'

CONVERSATIONS IN JUNE

'So the water... what makes it turn blue?'
'No idea,' Robin said. 'I'm not a scientist.'
I laughed. 'Don't get bitchy.'
'I was only kidding.'
'I know.'
'I'm happy now I think,' Robin said.
'I'm glad you're alright,' I said.
'I've really missed you, Will.'
'I should've come down sooner,' I said.
'Don't worry. I'm not trying to make you feel bad. But I really have missed you. Sometimes it's hard to get up in the morning and do the same things over and over. I have no time to think anymore. It drives me insane. I reckon you got here just in time.'
'Were you going to have a breakdown?'
'I don't know,' Robin said. 'Jordan and Abby have been a handful lately.'
'Forget about them for now,' I said. 'This is our time. Forget about Jordan. He's fast asleep.'
'I know,' Robin said. 'Thanks.'

At last we came to the glowing surf. The sand behind us was grey and the sea was as black as the night sky. I looked at Robin as we stared into the phosphorescent water. Her face was blue and her eyes were like white pearls.

'You're glowing,' Robin said to me.
'So are you,' I said. 'You suit being blue.'

'So do you.'

'Oh no,' I said. 'I hate Smurfs.'

We sat on the sand.

'It's so nice out here,' I said. 'I wish I could afford to live here.'

'It's not always as pretty as this. Most of the time you can't see it.'

I shrugged. 'But in the morning it's all here when you wake up.' Then I said in a mocking voice: 'Step right up — down here's paradise on earth! Look at the beach. Look at the harbour. Look at the boats going in and out of the town. Look at all the pretty things. There's so much to see!'

'Don't be naïve, Will. You know for a fact it isn't always calm here. A lot of the time it's more like "Look at all the fucking tourists!"'

I laughed and rocked back on the sand. Robin laughed after me.

'It's so quiet,' I said after laughing.

'You sound surprised. You've been down here before, you know. At night. Remember the last time you were here?'

'No,' I said. 'When was the last time we came down here this late?'

'A part of me doesn't want to say. It was a fairly long time ago, let's put it that way.'

'How long?' I asked. 'Give me a clue.'

CONVERSATIONS IN JUNE

'Just after Abigail was born,' Robin said. 'You were with Chelsea at the time, and Mum and Dad were still alive. Sorry to mention Chelsea like that.'

'It's alright. That really was a long time ago.'

'Yeah, that's right,' Robin said.

'Was it really that long ago?' I asked.

'It was.'

I shook my head.

'Summer nights out here always remind me of our parents,' Robin said in a quiet voice. 'I miss them so much.'

'I know.' I put my arm around her. She rested her head on my shoulder.

'The pain never leaves you, does it?'

'No,' I said. 'It doesn't. I wish there was something I could do to take it all away from you.'

'I wish I could take it away from you too,' Robin said. 'It's hell on earth.'

'It is,' I said. 'We just have to be happy with what we have.'

'Yes. I suppose so.'

'You have your home here by the sea. You have your job and your daughter and Jordan, as much as he can be difficult. And I have my job in the café. I have good friends and a car. And I have plenty of money saved up in case we need it. Those are all reasons for us to keep fighting.'

'I know,' Robin said. 'But why did it have to happen to us? Why? That's all I want to know.'

'If I had the answer I'd tell you. Just be thankful we still have each other. And you have Abigail, too. She's happy and healthy and full of life.'

Robin smiled. 'I can tell you're happy, Will. I didn't quite believe you earlier but I think I'm certain of it now.'

'What do you mean? How can you tell?'

'I can just feel it. You make me happy when you say nice things, and you always say nice things when you're happy.'

'It's just the sea air,' I smiled.

'No. It's you. You make me happy.'

'Thank you. I wish I could make you happier.'

'I know,' Robin said.

'I wish there was a way to bring our parents back but there isn't. I wish they could see how strong you've become. I wish they could see how far the two of us have travelled together. And more than anything in the world I wish they could see how much your daughter has grown. I'd give anything, Robin, for them to be able to see her again, even for a brief moment.'

'Oh Will. I know.'

I sighed. I felt awful for saying those things.

CONVERSATIONS IN JUNE

'I'll stop being glum now,' I said. 'Let's talk about something more cheerful. I don't want to see you upset. That's not why I came here.'

'It's okay,' Robin said. 'I like it when we talk about these things. I'm not sure why. I just do. I'm pretty bad at talking to other people about it but with you it's okay.' She smiled. 'Only you make things truly okay.'

'Thanks. Now come on. Let's talk about nice things. Happy things like you were saying before. Because I'm not sure I can continue talking about death.'

'I'm sorry.'

I rested my chin on her head. 'Enough being sorry,' I said.

RICHARD ANDERSON

JUNE 25th

When I finished work I headed across the street to the Late House Café for something to drink. Harry was inside when I arrived. He was sitting by the window. The sun was on him and his head was down. I knocked on the table and he looked up and rubbed his red eyes. I sat down.

'Oh. Hello. How's it going?' he asked.

'Not bad,' I said. 'I'm tired though.'

'You're always tired,' Harry said.

'It seems that way.' I sat back and examined his face. 'How are you anyway?'

'I'm alright.'

'You looked troubled when I came in. Is everything okay?'

'Swell,' Harry said. He looked out of the window at the street. The market was closing. People were leaving the town. The owners of the stalls were stacking everything they hadn't sold into large boxes.

'Was work good?' I asked.

'It was the same as always.'

'Nothing bad to report?'

'Nothing,' Harry said.

'No issues with the manager today?' I asked.

'No. I didn't see him today.'

CONVERSATIONS IN JUNE

'Lucky.' I started to get up. 'I won't be a minute. Just getting a drink.'

While at the counter I looked across at Harry. His legs were crossed and his left hand was on his chin. His other hand was on his lap. I wondered what he was thinking about, sitting there with the slant of the afternoon sun across his face.

'You alright?' I asked when I came back.

'Yeah.'

'What are you thinking about?'

'Leaving my job. I want something different.'

'I knew there was something,' I said.

'Yeah, well, I've been doing the same thing for too long now, haven't I? Besides I can't stand it in there anymore.'

'How long has it been?' I asked.

'Five years,' Harry said. 'That's long enough for me. I can't tolerate it anymore.'

'I've heard this from you before,' I said.

'Well this time I mean it. I'm going to start looking for something soon. Anything. I'll move if I have to.'

'Just take it easy,' I said. 'You'll get there.'

He shrugged and mumbled something.

'Want to do something tonight?' I asked.

'We can do,' Harry replied. 'Why? Are you bored? Got some money?'

'I'm bored,' I said. 'And I can't stand being in the apartment with Isaac. He drives me crazy.'

'Is he still miserable about Charlotte?'

'Yeah,' I said. 'He won't shut up about her. I keep telling him to get over her but he won't listen. He just whines about how much he loves her. I swear I can hear him crying into his pillow every night.'

'Well she's gone and he can't have her back.'

'It's hard to tell him that when he doesn't listen,' I said.

'He's funny,' Harry said. He sat back and smirked. He looked better now.

'Isaac's misfortunes bring out the worst in us.'

'Yeah,' Harry said. 'They certainly do.'

'Some people don't go well together,' I said. 'You and Isaac don't go well together at all.'

Harry nodded. 'When I'm having a bad day I just remember that it could be worse,' he grinned, 'I could always be Isaac.'

'That's an ugly thing to say,' I said. 'What's made you so rotten today?'

'I'm always rotten.'

'These days you are,' I said.

'All days.'

I drank my coffee. 'Well he's up in the apartment at the moment. God knows what he's doing with himself up there. Probably mas –'

CONVERSATIONS IN JUNE

'Yeah alright, enough,' Harry said.

'We should go up and see him,' I joked.

'Not a chance,' Harry said.

'Why not?'

'I can't stand him. If I go up there now, in the mood I'm in... God knows what'll happen.'

'Let's go out and get food,' I said.

'Steak.' Harry suggested. 'How about steak? I haven't had steak in a while.'

'Steak sounds good to me. I haven't eaten since breakfast.' I paused. 'I think I'll go down to Sophia's later on and stay the night.'

'Sounds better than being with Isaac. Why don't you stay with Sophia all the time?'

'I don't know,' I said. 'I don't think she likes it when I'm around all the time. It spoils the mood between us.'

'Having trouble?' Harry asked.

'No. Not that I'm aware of.'

I began to think.

'Don't think,' Harry said.

'How'd you know I was thinking?'

'I can tell,' Harry said. 'When you're thinking your eyes change. They stare. And they go cloudy and your jaw loosens up and your eyebrows –'

'Okay, okay. What were we talking about?'

'Going out and eating,' Harry said.

'Oh yeah. The steakhouse down the street?'

'Sure.'

'Want to go now?' I asked.

'Let's finish these drinks first.'

'Alright.'

We drank slowly and talked very little. I had one mouthful of coffee left in my cup when Charlotte came into the café. We were both quite surprised. Pleasantly surprised, of course.

'Hello fellas,' she said. She pulled up a chair and sat down.

'Hello,' I said. 'What brings you in here this afternoon?'

'Oh,' she waved her hand, 'nothing.'

'Are you alright?'

'Yes, Harry, I'm quite alright,' Charlotte said. She crossed her legs and looked out of the window.

'How are things now that you and Isaac are finished?' I asked. 'Sorry for being so broad.'

'Oh, I don't care what you ask me,' she said. 'It was bound to come up at some point. And I'm fine. Thank you for asking. And I mean it, too.'

'I'm sorry,' I said.

'Don't be sorry,' Charlotte said. 'No hard feelings. I'm over it. I was over him before I left him.'

'Do you hate him?' I asked her.

'No,' Charlotte said. 'He's just too much.'

'Are we too much?' I asked.

'No. You're both quite funny.'

'Let's not talk about Isaac,' Harry said. 'He makes me want to punch something.'

'Have you two finished for the day?' Charlotte asked. We nodded. She looked at me. 'Why aren't you drinking for free in The Frog?'

She seemed disgusted that I should be drinking in a café that wasn't the one I worked in.

'Because I'm always there,' I said. She smiled. Harry offered to buy her a drink. She said she'd have a large mocha with whipped cream. He got up to get it.

'Has Harry had any luck with that girl he's been seeing?' Charlotte asked me.

'That Hayley girl?'

'Yes.'

'I don't know,' I said. 'He doesn't talk about her and I don't ask him. You know what he's like. He's quite closed about things like that.'

'But you're both close friends. Why shouldn't you talk about things like that?'

'I don't know,' I said.

'I suppose it's a thing with you men. Not talking and all that.'

'Yeah, it is. We're pretty shit.'

'You can talk to me whenever you want to, though,' Charlotte said. 'You know that, don't you?'

'I do,' I said. 'Thanks.'

'So when does Sophia go to Canada?'

'At the end of June next year,' I said. 'She'll be over there with her parents for a whole year.'

'Don't look so glum, Will. She'll be fine. She loves you now and she will love you when she comes back.'

'I know,' I said. 'I'll just miss her. That's all.'

Harry returned to the table. Charlotte thanked him for the drink. 'Shall we go for real drinks after this?' Charlotte asked.

'We were talking about getting steaks,' I said.

'Brilliant idea,' Charlotte said, smiling. 'I'll come with you if you don't mind.'

'Do you even like steak?' I asked.

'Of course I do. Why? Am I not allowed steak? Is it not ladylike enough? Is it too masculine? A big slab of meat on a plate? Too much for a woman?'

Harry laughed. Then we all laughed.

'No, not at all,' I said.

'I bet it's been a while since you've had a decent slab of meat anyway,' Harry said.

'Don't be so revolting, Harry.' The corners of Charlotte's eyes wrinkled and she smiled, showing all her straight white teeth.

'I'm right though, aren't I?' Harry said.

'Oh stop it now.'

Harry laughed.

'You two love to make a girl feel awkward.'

'Don't bring me into this,' I said. 'All I did was ask if you liked steak. I never doubted you.'

'I can handle a steak as well as anyone else,' Charlotte said. 'I'll show you.'

'Come on then,' I said. 'Drink up and we'll go to the steakhouse.'

'Give me a minute, Will. Good God.' Charlotte sipped her drink. 'I'm not even hungry yet.'

'It's half price until seven,' Harry said.

'We have plenty of time,' Charlotte said.

When we finished our drinks we left the café and started to the steakhouse. A man lying in the gutter begged us for change. I gave him a couple of copper coins and he thanked me.

Opposite the steakhouse was the Alpine Club.

'Can we go in there after our food?' Charlotte asked. She sounded keen.

'Sure,' I said. 'We'll get drunk.'

'I'll come too,' Harry said. 'I don't feel like going home early tonight.'

Once we had eaten we went to the Alpine Club to get drunk. It was dark inside and warm. We sat at the bar and shared a bottle of wine. The wine was red. I wasn't a fan of it so I ordered a whiskey and Coke and drank quickly to get pie-eyed.

For most of our time in Alpine Harry talked about Isaac. He brought up a number of points from a conversation he'd had with Isaac a couple of days before. 'You ought to fall in love with something you can't lose' was one thing he had said. And 'Relationships are not all that. Being in a relationship doesn't change anything. You still wake up the same person with the same problems, the same friends, the same job ... Everyone is hurt in some way ... You should get over her ... No-one will ever *truly* love you...' Then he started going on about all the women he had slept with over the years. 'Some of them stay with you,' he was saying. 'They stay in your head, and if you're not careful they can get into your heart. That's when things become dangerous. Because getting them out of your heart requires you to be a complete and utter whore to yourself. You should never fall in love. It's bad for your health.'

This bilge went on for quite some time. When he stopped talking we left the Alpine Club and went across town to another bar called the Cobra. We stayed in the Cobra for the rest of the night. In the Cobra we talked about going on vacation.

'I've been thinking about going abroad somewhere hot,' Harry said. 'What do you guys think?'

'I'd love to,' I said.

CONVERSATIONS IN JUNE

'Sounds good,' Charlotte said. 'But when?'

'Sometime next summer.'

'Where do you have in mind?' I asked.

In the end we agreed that Greece would be the best place to visit. Charlotte knew Greece well. She had been there on several occasions. She knew an island close to the mainland called Thasos. 'It's a wonderful place,' she assured us. 'Plenty to do. Plenty to see. It's quite big, too.'

Harry said that Thasos would be perfect. We were all pretty drunk at this point. I was thinking about Sophia. I missed her. I missed her badly because I was drunk. I hated to get drunk and miss her. It was like I didn't have her at all. She was not there with me. I wanted her to be. I really did.

The bar closed at three o'clock. Charlotte got a taxi home. Harry went with her. I walked to my apartment in the dark under the yellow streetlights. Isaac was asleep on the couch when I got back. He had been drinking. I woke him up.

'Charlotte…' he muttered.

'Hey,' I said, 'what are you doing on the couch?'

'What time is it?'

'Early morning. Almost four.'

'Oh shit.' He got up and rubbed his face with his hands. 'Sorry, Will. Are you alright?'

RICHARD ANDERSON

'Yeah. I'm good.'
'What's wrong?'
'Nothing,' I lied.
'You going to bed?'
'Yeah. I'm tired.'
'Where've you been?'
'Drinking. And thinking.'
'Same.'
'Let's not talk,' I said. 'Let's go to bed.'
'Alright. See you in the morning.'
'Goodnight Isaac.'

CONVERSATIONS IN JUNE

" "

THE SECOND YEAR
JUNE 2nd

'Oh for the love of God!' a voice cried from inside the restaurant. 'I'll kill them! I'll *kill* them!'

I stopped outside with my hands in my pockets. 'What's been going on here, Sands?' I asked.

The restaurant looked as if it had been ransacked by a gang of ruthless thugs.

Sands came outside. 'Are you kidding me?' he said. 'Didn't you see what just happened?'

'No. I didn't see anything.'

'This is the third time this month,' Sam Sanderson, or Sands as we called him, said. 'I'm going to go crazy. This is costing me too much money.'

'What's caused it?'

'Goats, Will. Goats. They come over from that field across the road and cause absolute havoc.'

'Why don't you put up a fence to stop them coming in? They won't bother you then.'

Sands rubbed his forehead. 'Ah, it's all money, Will. And I've got no time to be putting up fences.'

'Gee, Sands. I'd do it for you.'

'Would you really, Will?'

'Yeah. Sure. Why not.'

Sands put his hand on his chin. 'Nah. Thanks for the offer though. I don't want to labour you. I'm sure you've got enough on your plate. Hell knows I've got a lot on mine.'

'Good,' I said. 'Stops you going mad.'

'Isn't it a mess?'

I looked around the restaurant. 'Yeah. Looks like a hurricane's hit.'

'If I see them again I'll swing for them.'

I laughed. 'You'll swing for a bunch of goats?'

'Yes. I'm good in a fistfight.'

'Goats are strong, you know. And punching animals is cruel no matter what they do to you.'

'I can fight anything. I once wrestled a crocodile at a zoo in the Algarve. Believe me I did.'

'I believe it,' I said.

Sands shook his head. 'Those rotten beasts. Look at this place.'

There were upturned tables, broken chairs, smashed plates, bent forks, curved knives, ripped tablecloths. It was an ugly sight.

'There's plenty of driftwood at my sister's place,' I said. 'And I can get nails for nothing. We'll have a fence up in no time if you just let me.'

CONVERSATIONS IN JUNE

'Driftwood's nice. It's nice to look at and a joy to work with. Why are we so attracted to driftwood?'

'I think you nailed it already. Pardon the pun.'

'You don't have to make me a fence, Will.'

'I'll make it,' I said.

'Are you sure?' Sands asked. 'Really sure?'

'Yeah,' I said. 'Fuck it.'

'You're a swell guy, Will.'

'Don't kiss ass. It's alright.'

'How's it going with your girl?'

'We're getting on well thanks,' I said.

This was not entirely true.

'That's great to hear,' Sands said. 'Come by the restaurant sometime and I'll let you have the lunch menu. That's if you come in the evening of course.'

'That's kind of you,' I said. 'I'll bring her down here tomorrow. We're staying with my sister.'

'How is she?'

'She's quite stressed at the moment,' I said.

'I saw her last week but she didn't see me.'

'I apologise on her behalf,' I said.

Sands smiled, showing all his bad teeth, and shook his head. 'No need for that,' he said. 'They come here from time to time, you know. To eat. Sometimes Jordan stays behind. He drinks and we talk. He tells me how he can't play football anymore. Say, Will, what exactly happened to him?'

'He lost his foot in a boating accident,' I said.

'Good God. How did he manage that?'

'Got it caught in the engine is what he told me. He had to cut it off.'

Sands put his hand over his mouth. 'Good Christ,' he said. 'No wonder he's always drunk.'

'That doesn't sound good,' I said. 'You know he can still play football, don't you? Have you told Robin how bad he gets when he's here?'

'No. I haven't said a word.'

'What does he say when he's here?' I asked.

'He just bitches about how he's no longer a "real man." He says he's too embarrassed to play football without his best foot. He curses it all the time. He gets real rotten. Real nasty. It's bad for business. Last month he flipped a table, Will. He flipped a table and he was crying and throwing himself around and giving me all kinds of crap.'

'He wasn't with Robin, was he?'

'No,' Sands said. 'He was with one of his friends from that sports club he goes to sometimes.'

'I see. Was my niece there?'

'No, Will, she wasn't there. Don't worry. I rarely see them together.'

'Alright. Thanks for telling me. I'm pretty certain Robin doesn't have a clue what he gets up to when she's not around. I'll have a talk with him.'

'Jordan is a loose cannon,' Sands warned. 'Be careful. Approach him with caution.'

'I know him well enough,' I said. 'Thanks anyway. It's Abigail and Robin I'm concerned about.'

Sands nodded. 'I saw you walk down here before the goats attacked,' he said. 'What were you doing?'

'I just went to the shop,' I said. 'I'm on my way back now. We're having a party.'

'One with music and dancing you mean?'

'No. Just a quiet party. Just the five of us.'

'You should come down for a drink later,' Sands said. 'I'll have the place fixed up by then.'

'I'll mention it. I'll see you later, Sands.'

'See you later Will.'

I walked out of the restaurant and continued up the road to my sister's house.

'Don't let him give you trouble,' Sands shouted. I turned around. He was waving to me.

'I won't, Sands. I promise.'

'And don't let him hurt that sweet little niece of yours. If he touches her so help me God I'll go up there myself and get him like I got that crocodile.'

'Sure thing,' I said. 'Did you really wrestle a crocodile in the Algarve?'

'I did, Will. Don't you believe me?'

'I just find it difficult to imagine.'

Sam's face swelled like a toad. 'I'll show you what I can do one of these days,' he said. 'We'll go into town and beat up them Aston twins. Then you'll see how well I can hold up in a fight.'

I continued up the road and raised my hand. 'Goodbye Sands,' I said, smiling so hard that it hurt the corners of my mouth.

'Yes-yes. Catch you later, Will. Have a good party tonight and come down if you can.'

~

'Where the hell have you been?' Jordan asked as I stepped up to the patio.

'I lost track of time,' I said.

'Come and sit down. We'll put the food on now you're back. What do you want?'

'I'll just have the lobster,' I said.

'Nothing else?'

'No. Just the lobster.'

'I'll have the lobster too,' Sophia said.

'Okay then,' Jordan said. 'Get yourselves something to drink and we'll eat.'

We got our food. It smelled delicious. We ate at a big table outside in the sun. It was really a fine meal. The lobster was tender and every bite tasted like the sea.

CONVERSATIONS IN JUNE

By eight o'clock Abigail was fast asleep. According to Jordan she had been tired all day. Once Robin had put her to bed we sat in a circle on the patio. It was warm. We watched the sun behind the fading, orange clouds. I had a drink on my lap. Sophia was beside me. I had my arm around her. She had a glass of red wine in her hand.

'What a lovely evening this has been,' Robin said. 'It couldn't have gone better. It's great to be here as a family.'

I suspected she was a little drunk. 'True,' I said. 'The food was amazing. We should stay over more often.'

'You don't have to leave tonight you know,' Jordan said. 'Stay for breakfast. Both of you. What do you think, Sophie?'

I wanted to smack him. He had an ugly habit of calling Sophia *Sophie*, especially when he was drunk.

'What do you think, Sophia?' Robin asked.

Sophia was drifting off.

'We can stay,' she said quietly.

'Okay,' Robin said.

'Get more alcohol,' Jordan said. He raised his glass. He had his artificial foot on one of the vacant chairs. 'Come on, quick-quick.'

Robin went into the house and came out with a bottle of champagne and champagne glasses.

'What the hell do you think you're doing?' Jordan said. He looked appalled.

'What?' Robin asked, surprised.

'What are you doing with that champagne?'

'Won't you drink champagne?'

'I don't *want* champagne. I don't care for it.'

Robin shrugged. 'Why not?'

'We're not having champagne. You know I don't like that shit. Bring out some beer. Bring out the liquor. Do you like champagne, Will?'

I grunted. I didn't want to say that I did.

'Do you like it, Sophie?'

Sophia shrugged. I felt embarrassed.

Jordan waved his hand. 'Go put it back in the kitchen,' he said. 'And get the beer and liquor. This isn't one of your fancy business occasions now.' He laughed. 'No-one here's in a suit. No-one here has a title. Go in and get some *real* alcohol.'

Robin went inside. When she came out she had a case of beer and two bottles of whiskey. She opened the whiskey straightaway, refilled our glasses, added Coke, ice, and then forced a cold beer into Jordan's big hand.

'Are we all happy now?' Jordan asked. I nodded. Sophia nodded. Robin didn't respond at all. She was holding her glass with both hands and staring into the trees.

CONVERSATIONS IN JUNE

'It's been a good day,' I said. After saying this I felt guilty and a little stupid. I glanced at my sister.

'Thank you both for coming,' she said.

'It isn't over yet,' Jordan said. 'We've got the rest of the night.'

I couldn't tell whether Jordan was happy or just pretending to be happy. He sat back and turned his head to the trees. 'This place makes me think of all the wonders of the world.' No-one said anything so Jordan went on. 'How about we go on holiday somewhere?'

Robin shook her head. 'Where?' she said.

'Anywhere,' Jordan boomed. 'We could go to France, we could go to Greece, we could go to Amsterdam, to Brussels, to Africa, America, South America... India, China, Japan.' His excitement swelled with every country he named.

'Sophia's going to Canada for a year at the end of this month,' I said. 'So she can't go. And I'm going away with my friends in September.'

Jordan ignored me. 'What about Italy?' he said. 'We could go to Rome. Castel Sant'Angelo. The Colosseum. The Pantheon. The Vatican. The Spanish Steps. Ostia Antica.'

'It's a dream,' Robin said. 'We don't have the money. We can't afford a holiday and I can't get the time off work.'

'Now worries,' Jordan said. 'I'll just take some out of our savings and get a babysitter for Abby.'

Robin glared at him. 'You will *not*,' she said.

'Ah loosen up,' Jordan said. 'People our age travel up to three, four, maybe five times a year. I don't think they call them holidays come to think of it. I think they call them ventures. You see? We don't have to go for a fortnight. A weekend is fine.'

'But you just came back from Cornwall,' I said. I hated to bring it up because it meant talking about Jordan's accident.

'That was a terrible trip,' Jordan said. His face contorted. 'I'm never going there again. We won't talk about that here.'

'What will we talk about?' I asked.

'Going away for a couple of days between, say, now and this time next year,' Jordan said.

'Sophia goes away to Canada soon,' I repeated. I was getting bored of him. 'She won't be able to join us if we go away. And I'm going to Greece in September. I have no money left, not even for a weekend "venture."'

'He's right,' Sophia said.

Jordan sat back. He was thinking. 'Alright then,' he said after a moment. 'When you come back, Sophie, we'll all go away. Where do you want to go? You choose. Keep it simple. What about Spain?'

CONVERSATIONS IN JUNE

'I love the little towns out there,' Sophia said. 'I haven't been in years. Spain is lovely to paint.'

'People have painted that place a million times over,' Jordan said. His face contorted again. 'There's nothing out there that's original. You should paint something decent for a change.'

'Well maybe she'd like to paint Spain for herself,' I said. I put my hand over my aching eyes.

'You're the fuckin' same, Will. You and that novel of yours. It's no different than your other books. You're still not writing to change the world. Remember that talk we had last year?'

'I do,' I said.

'Write something worth reading!'

'Why don't you shut up, Jordan?' I said. 'And I think you should apologise to Sophia.'

He laughed aloud. 'For what?'

'For putting her down about her art,' I said.

'Oh, alright then, sorry. I was just saying you should paint something that hasn't been painted before. Paint something *different*.'

'Practically everything in the world has been painted,' Sophia said. 'Being different doesn't matter to me. I enjoy what I do. I don't need to paint something unique to feel good about my art.'

Jordan mumbled and drank. He unbuttoned his shirt and let his stomach roll over his belt.

'So is it going to be Spain?' he asked.

'I don't know,' I said. 'I don't care either.'

'We aren't going anywhere,' Robin said.

'You fucking miserable bitch,' Jordan said.

I stood up. 'Don't you talk to her like that,' I said. 'Who the hell do you think you are?'

'Hey, wow,' Jordan said. 'Sit down, Will.'

'You take it back right now,' I said.

'Alright, alright.' Jordan raised his open hands in surrender. 'I take it back. Happy now?'

'Apologise,' I said.

'I'm sorry, Robin,' Jordan said. He still sounded reluctant.

'And apologise to Sophia. Properly this time.'

He looked at Sophia. 'I'm sorry, Sophie.'

'It's *Sophia*,' I snapped. '*S-o-p-h-i-a*.'

'Okay. *Sophia*. I'm sorry.'

Sophia said nothing.

'You need to calm down, Will,' Jordan said. 'Why not put more ice in your drink?'

'No. I don't want any fucking ice.'

'Alright, alright. I was only suggesting.'

I sat down. I could feel my heart beating hard behind my chest.

'Enough now,' Robin said. 'We're not going anywhere. Both of you just pack it in, please. I'm tired of all this fighting.'

CONVERSATIONS IN JUNE

Jordan sat forward. 'No-one's fighting,' he said, pretending to look confused. He had the most irritating smirk on his face. 'Are we fighting, Will?'

I kept quiet. I wanted to get up and leave.

'Ah, pass me some of that whiskey, will you?' Jordan asked me. For some reason I handed it to him. He snatched it out of my hand. 'What a dive this evening has taken. How about we go and see Sands?'

'I won't go,' Robin said. 'I'm staying right here. I have to be here for Abigail.'

'Fine,' Jordan huffed. 'You stay here and be lonely. We don't need you around to have fun.'

'Fuck off,' Robin said, and she raised two fingers at him. Jordan sniggered like a child.

'Ooh,' he said, 'there's no need for that.'

'I'm staying right here,' she insisted.

'Fine,' Jordan said. 'What about it then, Will? Sophie? Sorry. *Sophia.*'

'I'll stay behind with Robin and Abby,' Sophia said. 'I'm too tired to go down to the restaurant.'

'Sounds alright to me,' I said. I was thinking.

'It'll be nice just the two of us,' Robin said. She looked better now but only a little.

'A night out for the boys then,' Jordan said, rubbing his hands together.

I stood up, finished my whiskey, and went into the kitchen for food. When I returned to the patio

Sophia and Robin were talking. Jordan was missing. I asked where he was.

'He's in the house changing.'

'Right,' I said. 'We'll go down when he's ready. While we're down there I'll try to sober him up. That's my plan.'

Robin brushed her hair back with her fingers. Her face was white. Sophia put her arm around her. 'I'm okay,' Robin said. Her hand was over her eyes.

'Relax for the night,' I said. 'We'll go down and talk to Sands. He's a good guy. And he's concerned about you, Robin. He said so before.'

'Remind me to go down and see him soon.'

'We should go down in the morning,' I said.

'That's a lovely idea,' Sophia said. 'We can have breakfast and head out to the beach afterwards.'

Robin didn't seem sure.

'Are you two alright?' I asked.

'Yeah,' Sophia answered. 'We'll be fine.'

'I'll talk to Jordan,' I said. 'Well, I'll try.'

~

We sat at a table in the middle of the restaurant. It was dark and the lights above the entrance were flickering. There were candles on every table. Sam Sanderson was at the bar speaking to an elderly couple. The elderly couple were talking about Africa. The old man looked sad. His head was in his hands. He was telling Sands that he was too sick to travel. 'I am very sick,' he was saying. Sands suggested he go to one of the local zoos. 'It is not the same,' the old man said. 'And it is not all about seeing Africa again,' he added.

When they left I felt melancholy. I bought a bottle of wine and drank it steadily. Jordan was drinking whiskey. We were not talking. Sam Sanderson started playing the piano. From time to time he would go behind the bar and take a drink. No goats tonight, I thought, staring across the road into the trees. It's too late for them now.

'This has turned out to be quite a dull night,' Jordan said slowly. He was tapping his glass with his fingers.

'What's the matter? I asked. 'You were happy before. Well you looked it.'

'I wasn't happy. Not at all. It was all a front.'

I said nothing.

'I was simply enjoying myself,' Jordan said.

'Isn't that the same as being happy?' I said.

'No,' Jordan said. 'You can be very unhappy and still have a good time.'

'I guess so.'

I sat back.

'Play something good on that piano, Sands.'

'I only know sad tunes,' Sands said.

'For God's sake,' Jordan sighed.

'Calm down,' I said.

'I am calm.'

'I'll play something sad but a little quicker and see how it goes,' Sands said.

'Go ahead,' Jordan said. 'Do whatever you want. Can I light a cigarette?'

'Yeah, alright.'

Jordan lit a cigarette and sat back. He blew the smoke up in the air and put his head down. I continued to drink. We were the only people in the restaurant. I had some bread and spread butter on it. The bread had little seeds stuck down on the crusts.

'Have some of this bread,' I said. I offered the plate to Jordan. 'It's actually alright, even with these little seeds.'

Jordan tore a piece of the bread and put it in his mouth. 'Hack – it's dry,' he said.

'Have some water.'

I called for a glass of water. Sands brought it from the back. Jordan drank it. He drank the whole glass. It was good to see him drink it.

'Better?' I asked.

'A little,' he said. 'Want a cigarette?'

'Sure,' I said.

We smoked together.

CONVERSATIONS IN JUNE

'You're alright you know, Will,' Jordan said.
'Thanks. What makes you say that?'
'Because I'm sorry.'
'Sorry?'
'For my behaviour earlier.'
'It's alright,' I said.
'No. It isn't.'
I said nothing.
'You know it isn't alright,' Jordan said.
'Don't talk about it,' I said.
'I have to.'
'No, you don't have to,' I said. 'We don't have to do anything right now.'
'Alright.'
'Are you feeling better now you've apologised?' I asked.
'A little. I'm still drunk though.'
'You've had a lot tonight. Is there any reason?'
'There're many reasons,' Jordan said.
'What's the main reason?'
He lifted his leg and slammed his artificial foot down on the chair opposite.
'I'm sorry,' I said.
'Don't be. It wasn't your fault.'
He put his leg down.
'It could've been worse,' I said. As soon as I said this I felt like an idiot.

'Yeah. I know.'

I turned to Sands. 'Play something a bit slower,' I said.

'Right on,' he said. He cracked his fingers and went on playing.

'I wish I could do something like that,' I said.

'You can write,' Jordan said.

'I can't write as well as he can play.'

Jordan shrugged. His head was tilted to the side. 'You're published, aren't you?'

'You know I am,' I said.

'So someone thought you were good at what you do. See. I can talk all wise and shit sometimes.'

I wasn't sure how wise it was.

'Thanks. But I'm critical of my own work. It's an artist thing I suppose. I'm not sure.'

Jordan lit another cigarette. 'An *artist* thing,' he said slowly, as if dissecting the word. 'An *artist*. I was an artist once, Will.' He blew out a cloud of smoke. 'I was like you once. Every day I was a pro. Every day I was a champion. I'd run out there, onto the pitch, and I'd play like a god.'

'I'm sorry,' I said.

'Don't be sorry, Will.'

'I just feel bad.'

'Whatever.'

'You can still play you know,' I said.

CONVERSATIONS IN JUNE

'People keep telling me,' Jordan said.

'Well you can.'

'What if I don't want to play?'

'You shouldn't limit yourself,' I said.

'You don't know what it's like.'

I shrugged.

'Time slowed down and something within me flew away,' Jordan said. 'I'm not much of a man now. In fact I'm less than a man.' I looked at him. He was almost crying. His hand was over his mouth. 'Do you know what it's like to wake up in the night screaming?'

I said I didn't.

'No. Of course you don't. You don't have anything to scream about. Try to imagine this, Will. Try to imagine losing your hands in some horrific accident. Imagine not being able to do that which you were born to do. Life isn't worth living if you can't do what you love.'

'Do you want to die?' I asked.

He nodded, then shook his head.

'You have a daughter,' I said. 'And you have Robin. We're all here for you. You don't want to die. That's crazy. It takes a lot more than a lost foot to make a man want to give up his life – his *entire* life. Don't talk so stupid.'

'I'm hollow without my sport, Will.'

'I told you. We have all told you. Even Sands has told you. You can still play football.'

'No,' Jordan said. 'That's all I'm saying. No.'

I shook my head.

'Don't you shake your head at me,' Jordan said, pointing. 'Can't you see it? Can't you see that I've been defeated?'

'No you haven't. Don't talk shit.'

'And what kind of a father am I now?' he said. 'Forget football for a minute. What kind of a father am I now? Look at me. I can't do *anything*.'

'Take it easy,' I said.

'Don't tell me to take it easy. You and your perfect life. You and your books.'

'My life isn't perfect,' I said.

'Oh don't give me that.'

'Relax,' I said. 'Remember you're drunk.'

'Don't talk to me.'

'Stop being such a child. Let me tell you something, Jordan. Listen to me. You think you have it bad, do you? You think you have it worse than everyone else, do you? Listen to me. I knew a man once. His name was Sydney, and he was a very nice, very caring human being. But one day he fell seriously ill. He had to have an operation. But the operation led to complications. Do you know what Crohn's disease is, Jordan?'

CONVERSATIONS IN JUNE

'No,' Jordan answered.

'Look it up sometime.' I sighed. 'Anyway, Sydney went very thin. He lost his appetite and suffered multiple heart attacks. Every day for him was a horrendous battle. I remember him crying one night when I came to visit. He was in the corner by his bed, wailing, saying that his life was over, and calling out in despair "Why did it have to be me, Will?" and "Will I ever be strong enough to hold my children again?" Keep in mind, Jordan, that this man had never done a thing wrong to anyone in his life. But I guess that's the way it is, isn't it? Anyway, he spent two long years wired to a bed because no-one at the hospital could figure out what the trouble was. And in the end they were too late.' I paused. 'Before any of this happened poor Sydney was at the top of his game. He was into his sport, like you. And he had a lot of friends, including me. And he had a girlfriend and two little boys. He had everything right there, and the thing is he knew it. He knew he had the world, and he was grateful every day. We used to tell him that he wasn't alone. But in the end that's exactly how he went. Alone in his bed, at four o'clock in the morning, with no-one by his side. We all felt like a bunch of liars, and we still do to this day. So don't ever say that you're defeated. Because you don't know what it means to be defeated. I understand that people experience things differently. But keep in mind that I have lost too, as well as my sister.'

Sands came up to the table.

'Are you boys alright?' he asked.

'Yeah,' I said.

'We're fine,' Jordan said.

Sands went to the bar and mixed himself a tall, icy cocktail. 'This one's for old Sands,' he said, winking at me, and returned to the piano. He began to play. Eventually he started to sing. As the night went on he became more confident and sang with his head thrown back, his eyes tight shut, and his fingers hard on the keys.

'Do you think he's drunk?' I asked Jordan.

'I don't know and I don't care.'

'Do you want to go yet?' I asked.

'No.'

It was almost three o'clock. I was tired. I wanted to go back to my sister's and crawl into bed with Sophia. I was missing her.

'I want to go soon,' I said.

'Go then. You are your own man. You can do whatever you want. You can have whatever you want. You can have the whole world.'

'Knock it off,' I said and stood up.

'Go on up to the house. I'll follow you.'

'Will you?' I asked.

CONVERSATIONS IN JUNE

'I will,' Jordan said.

'I don't believe you.'

'I'm not a child. I can take care of myself.'

'I don't care,' I said. 'You're pissed.'

'I'll follow you,' Jordan said. 'Just let me have one last drink.'

'No. You're coming home with me.'

'No, Will. I'll drink and sleep here.'

'This isn't a hotel. You'll leave with me.'

'Go to hell.'

'Do you think all this senseless drinking is going to help you become a better person?' I said. 'A better man? All it'll do is kill you.'

'What the hell do you know about drinking?' Jordan said. 'You don't know anything.'

'I know a lot of things. Now get up.'

'I'll be fine. Don't bother me.'

'Come on. Enough of this now.' I put my hand on his shoulder and he jolted.

'Don't you put your hands on me,' he said.

'We'll get a taxi.'

'Back off.'

I called Sands over.

'Trouble?'

'Call us a taxi,' I said.

'No problem,' Sands said. He scurried behind the bar and called for a taxi.

'If you weren't Robin's brother I'd have put you out by now,' Jordan grunted.

'I don't care,' I said.

'What do you mean?'

'I don't care what you think of me,' I said.

'You think you're better than me?'

'No. I just want you home. We'll be down here for breakfast in the morning so don't panic. Come home now and I'll forget this whole ordeal.'

Sands came back to our table. 'A taxi will be here for you in ten minutes,' he said.

'Doing breakfast tomorrow, Sands?' I asked.

'You bet. Will you be here?'

'Of course. We're going down to the beach afterwards. Apparently it'll be a scorcher tomorrow.'

'Are we really coming down here for breakfast in the morning, Will?' Jordan asked. Something in his voice had changed. There was no anger in it anymore. I was surprised.

'Yes. We are. We'll have sausage and bacon and eggs, and those funny little round potato things Sands makes with the chopped onions inside, and we'll have toast and cranberry juice in the sun and later we'll go down to the beach and roll around in the surf just like the old days. Won't it be nice?'

Jordan nodded. He was smiling. 'I'm sorry, Will. I'm really sorry.'

CONVERSATIONS IN JUNE

'Yeah. I know,' I said.

'I'd never hit you, Will. Not really. That was just talk. That's all I ever do is talk.'

'It's okay. Let's forget it now please.'

'You make me happy, you know. All of you.'

'Don't get like that,' I said. 'Not now.'

~

When we got back to the house I crept into the spare bedroom and crawled under the covers with Sophia. She stirred and opened her eyes.

'I'm sorry I woke you,' I said. The room was dark. I could barely see her. I took off the top part of my clothes and we kissed.

'What's the matter?' she asked.

'Nothing,' I said. I kissed her neck.

'You're not usually like this,' she said. She put her arms around me.

'It's nothing,' I said. 'I'm just happy to be back here with you.'

She smiled. 'Don't kid me, Will. What's the matter really?'

'Nothing.'

'Is Jordan alright?'

'He's fine. He's in bed.'

'He didn't get really drunk did he?'

'No, he was fine,' I said. 'Sands played the piano and sang and we had a good time.'

'Why are you being so?'

'So what?'

Sophia shrugged. 'Nothing. I love you.'

'I love you too.'

'Are you tired?' Sophia asked.

'No, not really,' I said. 'I don't want to sleep just yet. I'm a little restless for some reason.'

'Are you drunk?'

'No,' I said. 'You know when I'm drunk.'

'I can smell rose on you.'

'Sands had rose candles on the tables.'

'Was it busy down there?'

'There was an old couple at the bar,' I said.

'Did you talk to them?' Sophia asked.

'No,' I said. 'But Sands did. The old man was talking about Africa.'

'What was he saying?'

'He was telling Sands that he was too sick to go back there. He was crying. I've never seen an old man cry before.'

'Oh. That sounds awful,' Sophia said.

'His wife was very understanding,' I said.

'That's sweet.'

'He was just so, so sad.'

'Do you think he'll be well again someday?'

CONVERSATIONS IN JUNE

'I don't think so,' I said. 'I don't think he will ever be well again.'

'I wish things were not so cruel sometimes.'

'I know,' I said.

We kissed and I cuddled her from behind.

'I can feel your heart,' Sophia said.

'Sorry,' I said.

She turned to me.

'Want to talk?' she asked.

'I don't know. I was enjoying the silence.'

'That sounds mean,' Sophia said.

I grinned. 'I am mean.'

'Don't be silly.'

'I'm silly, too.'

I pinched the back of her leg.

'Stop it.' She laughed lightly through her nose. I felt her breath go down my chest.

'Was Robin okay?' I asked.

'She was fine. We talked and watched TV.'

'Was Abby alright?'

'Yes, she was fine.'

'Good.'

We stopped talking for a while. Sophia closed her eyes. I ran my fingers through her hair.

'I'll miss you,' I said.

'What?' Sophia said, coming back from somewhere far away.

'I said I'll miss you.'

'I'll miss you too,' Sophia said. 'Don't think about it. You don't have to think about it.'

'I do think about it though.'

'Don't worry. I love you and I'll be back.'

'Please come back,' I said.

'I promise I'll come back. I won't be gone forever. It'll be hard for me too you know.'

'I know. I'm just being soft.'

'You know how much I miss my parents,' Sophia said.

'I know.'

'I'll send you lots of pictures.'

'And postcards?' I said.

'Yes. I know how much you like postcards.'

'I wish I could come with you.'

'You have work though,' Sophia said.

'I hate it.'

'Don't you like coffee anymore?'

'I love coffee,' I said. 'But knowing you'll be over in Canada makes me hate it.'

'I'm sorry,' Sophia said.

'No. Don't be sorry.'

I kissed her. I felt a little foolish.

'I love you,' I said.

'Come on. I know you do. You don't usually say it this much. Is something bothering you?'

CONVERSATIONS IN JUNE

'I'll miss you. That's all.'
'Don't think about it, Will.'
'You'll be safe, won't you?'
'I will,' Sophia said. 'I'm always safe.'
'Because I can't protect you everywhere.'
'I don't always need protecting, Will.'
'I know. But…'
'I'm a grown woman.'
'That hurts.'
'What hurts?'
'Just the way you said that,' I said. 'It makes me feel unnecessary. Like you don't need me.'
'You know I couldn't live without you.'
'You could, I think. You're stronger than me.'
'We're both strong,' Sophia said.

We stopped talking. I felt embarrassed so I suggested we go to sleep.

'Alright. If you want to,' Sophia said.
'Do *you* want to?' I asked.
'Yes, Will, it'd be nice.'
'Okay,' I said. I got into a comfortable position and closed my eyes. 'Let's go to sleep and forget about you going away.'
'Right. Goodnight Will.'
'Goodnight Sophia.'

I kissed her cheek. When I woke up in the morning she was not there.

RICHARD ANDERSON

" "

THE HOLIDAY
SEPTEMBER 19th

It was hot and there was a light breeze coming in off the Aegean. Charlotte climbed on the back of my scooter and we started along the smooth, winding road out of the town. I could see Harry and Hayley behind me. There was a lot of black smoke coming out of the exhaust of their scooter. To our left were green mountains climbing up into the empty sky, and to our right was the turquoise sea. There were wide avenues cut between the trees to prevent forest fires from spreading. In the distance we could make out the mainland where we had flown in.

We stopped at a place called Skala Rachoníou and ate in an open café. It was hot. We had fried octopus and drank lots of water. It was a nice place and we could see the sea and it was very quiet.

'I wonder what's up in the mountains,' I said.
'Probably small villages,' Hayley replied.
'I couldn't live up there,' Harry said.

CONVERSATIONS IN JUNE

I lit a cigarette and gave one to Charlotte. 'Why not?' I asked.

'Too quiet,' Harry said.

'Too out of touch?'

'Yeah.'

'I'd give it a go,' I said.

'So would I,' Charlotte put in.

'When I'm rich I'll come back here,' I said.

Harry shook his head.

We paid for the food and drinks before we left. I led the way out of Skala Rachoníou. There was an old man in a ragged white shawl walking along the side of the road. He had a long, gnarled stick, and in front of him were about a dozen goats and some sheep. Harry almost hit a goat as we tried to get around. The old man didn't seem to care.

About a mile down the road Charlotte tapped me on the shoulder. I turned my head. 'What's wrong?' I said.

'I'm too hot and I want to do something. I want to be in the sea. Look at it, Will. Isn't it the most gorgeous thing you have ever seen?'

'Alright,' I said. 'We'll stop.'

We pulled into a place called Skala Kallirachi. There was a big harbour here and a small beach. We parked the bikes outside a café and sat in the shade with whiskey and Retsina. Retsina is Greek wine. We all liked it.

'We're roughly half way to Limenária,' Charlotte told us. 'It won't take us much longer to get there.'

'This island is pretty as hell,' Harry said. 'Look at all the boats. I wish I had a boat. Look at that big one with the tall mast.'

I looked at the big boat. It was nothing to me. It was just a boat.

'There're loads of boats in Thasos,' I told him.

'How's your bike?' Charlotte asked Harry. I handed her a cigarette and lit it for her.

'It's holding alright,' Harry answered.

'I hope it's comfortable for you, Hayley.'

'The smoke it produces is terrible,' I said.

'As long as it moves I don't care,' Hayley said. 'How's yours, Will?'

'It's fine.'

I sat back. Charlotte was staring out to sea. She looked very tan. Her cheeks were red and her hair was loose around her shoulders.

'Are you going to go for a dip in the surf?' I asked. 'There's a beach where we came in.'

'Yes,' Charlotte said, smiling. She finished her cigarette and got up. 'Are you coming for a swim, Hayley?'

CONVERSATIONS IN JUNE

'Yeah I'll come.'
'We'll see you boys there.'
The girls went down to the water.
'Are you alright?' Harry asked me.
'Just tired,' I said.
'You're not still glum are you?'
'I'll be honest. Yes. I am.'
'Don't think about it.'

I looked out. Charlotte and Hayley were playing on the beach. I could hear their laughter.

'Let's not talk about it,' I said.
'Don't look so down.'
'I can't help it.'
'You're making me feel terrible,' Harry said.
'I don't really care.'
'That's your problem. You don't care about anything anymore.'
'I'm having a good time,' I said.
'You're miserable.'
'No. I'm having a good time.'

Harry stood up. 'I'm going for a swim with the girls. Come with me if you want.' He slapped me on the shoulder. I watched him go over to the beach. Charlotte and Hayley had taken off most of their clothes and were laughing joyfully.

I got up, paid the bill at the café, and joined the others in the surf. The water was warm and clear. It was like walking into a bath.

We were the only people on the beach. The sand stuck to our arms and legs and since we had no towels we had to dry out in the sun. I was quiet while the others were talking.

'There's beer in my scooter,' Harry said. 'Who wants a bottle?'

'Warm beer?' Charlotte asked. 'Keep it for yourself. It's like gasoline anyway.'

'I have whiskey too,' Harry said. 'Want that?'

'I'll have some,' Hayley said.

'Fine. Go on then,' Charlotte said. 'Will you drink with us, Will?'

'Sure. I'll drink to Greece and all her fine boats and beaches and people.'

~

In an hour or so we dressed and continued to Limenária. My jeans were glued to my knees with sweat and my shirt was damp under my arms and around my neck. The girls were in loose clothes and Harry had unbuttoned his shirt. It flapped like a flag in the wind as we rode along.

CONVERSATIONS IN JUNE

'I'm worried about you,' Charlotte said in my ear. 'Tell me what's wrong.'

'Nothing's wrong,' I said.

'Don't be stubborn. Please tell me what's wrong. You've been down all day.'

'I'm trying to concentrate on the road.'

Ahead of us were two men riding donkeys. The donkeys were scruffy and covered in dust.

'I'm fine, Lottie. It's just the heat. It's been getting to me for days now. I thought I was going to be sick earlier on in the café.'

She rubbed my arm. For a moment I forgot all my problems. 'As long as you're sure,' she said. 'All your worries should be at home where they belong. I'm here for you if you want me.'

'I know,' I said. 'Thank you.'

The landscape to our left began to climb. After several miles we arrived at a place called Skala Marion. There were a lot of people here and I counted three tour buses.

When we got out of the village I noticed that Harry and Hayley were no longer behind us. I stopped by the side of the road. 'Wait here,' I said to Charlotte.

I walked back down the road to see if I could spot them. There was no sign of them anywhere.

'I hope they're okay,' Charlotte said. I climbed on the scooter and we rode back into Skala Marion.

'They've probably gone off the cliff,' I joked.

'They've most likely broken down, Will. There's always that.'

She was right. We found them outside a hotel. Harry was on his knees inspecting the bike. Apparently he had hurt his foot on the kick-start. Hayley was shaking her head.

'What's up with it?' Charlotte asked.

'Is it out of petrol?' I said.

'We lost power up that hill' – Harry pointed down the road into the town – 'and now the back wheel won't spin without my help.' He demonstrated by putting the scooter on its stand so that the back wheel was off the ground. He revved the engine. The little engine roared but the back wheel was not spinning. Then he nudged the wheel with his foot. The wheel started spinning but it was no use. We could all see that it was not powerful enough to shift the weight of the bike. 'I have no way of fixing it.'

I took a look under the scooter.

'What are you doing?' Harry said. 'You know nothing about motorcycles.'

'He's doing his best to have a look for you,' Hayley said.

CONVERSATIONS IN JUNE

Harry mumbled something under his breath and sat down on a rock by the side of the sandy road. Charlotte sat with him. 'It'll be alright,' she said.

'No,' Harry said. 'I think we're fucked.'

I sat on the bike and gripped the handlebars. 'What do we do?' I said. 'We can't just leave it here, can we?'

'Yes we can,' Harry said. 'I won't have something like this ruin the holiday.'

'Calm down,' I said. 'We have to think.'

'Let's leave the damn thing here,' Harry said.

'That's your money wasted then,' I said.

'I know but there's nothing I can do.'

'You still have money left, don't you?' Hayley asked. Harry put his hand over his face.

'I'll have to leave it here,' he said. 'Or we could wheel it out of town and put a sign on the seat saying FREE.'

'I don't think we have much of a choice,' Charlotte said. She was half-hearted about it.

Harry made a fist and put it to his forehead. 'What do we do about transport now? How are we going to get to Limenária?'

'You'll have to hail a cab,' I said.

'That's fine,' Hayley said. 'I'll go in a taxi any day. I don't mind.'

'I'll take Charlotte as normal,' I said.

Harry put his hands over his face. 'For God's sake. I don't believe this.'

No-one said anything for a while after that. I figured we were done for. Then, for no reason at all, a small jeep pulled up in front of us. At first I didn't think much of it. Then a man got out and came over to us. There was a woman with him. The woman was slender and dark and her hair was long to her chest and light brown. She had dark eyes and large square glasses. The man she was with was broad and wore sandals and a yellow T-shirt and khaki shorts.

'Bonjour,' the woman said to us. 'Are you having a problem? My name is Charlie.' She shook my hand before shaking everyone else's hands. 'And this is my brother. He is Anthony.'

We were all confused, hot, and frustrated.

'Yes,' I said, scratching my head. 'We *do* have a problem. My friend's bike has broken down and now we can't get to town.'

Charlie glanced at the bike with her hands on her hips. '*Merde*,' she said. 'It looks awfully old.'

'I bought it cheap,' Harry said.

Charlie shook her head. 'Shame,' she said. 'Is the other bike working?'

'Yes,' I said. 'It's working fine.'

'Where are you going to?'

'Limenária,' I said.

CONVERSATIONS IN JUNE

'We are going there too,' the French girl said. 'Would you like to join us?'

Hayley and Harry looked at each other with their eyebrows raised. We were all quite unsure.

'That's kind of you,' Harry said. He was not angry now. 'We appreciate the offer but we don't even know you.'

'Are you sure?' I asked Charlie. I'd had enough of Harry at this point. I figured that ignoring him was the best thing to do.

'Do not worry,' Charlie said. 'I don't mind.'

'We have some money,' Hayley said.

'No, no charge. You are holidaying?'

'Yes,' Harry said. 'It's been great until now.'

Charlie nodded at her brother and said something to him in French. We all looked at her suspiciously. We talked a little about the bikes and where we had bought them from. The French girl did not look impressed. She said we should have rented instead. Harry looked displeased. He was quite embarrassed because he knew we had made the wrong decision. I was the lucky one. My scooter still worked.

'I'll follow on my bike,' I said, shrugging. 'What's the best thing to do with this one?'

'Leave it here,' Charlie shrugged. 'No-one will care. Someone will take it.'

We left the bike by the side of the road. Harry put the keys on the seat and the broad man named Anthony helped Hayley into the jeep.

'This is all quite sudden and strange,' I said to Charlotte. 'Do you think we can trust them?'

'Oh, I don't care,' she said. 'I'm too hot to care. But did you see the way she glared at us?'

Charlie and the others set off to Limenária after a short conversation about something, I forget what. I started the bike and we followed them. Charlie was driving. I could see her hair flying back in the cool wind.

~

The drive to Limenária was short and I thought I was going to faint. I cursed the sun for being in my eyes and the heat for burning my head. When we arrived I followed Charlie through the streets of the town. I noticed there were plenty of cafés and a few small restaurants scattered here and there. This made me feel at ease. The streets of Limenária reminded me of the streets of Liménas. The buildings were tall and white with red roofs and blue shutters.

'Thank you for the drive,' Hayley said to the French couple.

'No problem, no problem,' Charlie said.

CONVERSATIONS IN JUNE

'What's in this town?' Harry asked.

'There is a good bar near the waterfront,' said the French girl. 'This evening there will be music. We are going to see it.'

'Sounds good,' I said. 'Do we owe you anything for your help?'

'No,' Charlie said. 'You owe us nothing.'

'What do we think about going to this bar?' I asked the group. The girls shrugged.

'What do you think, Charlotte?' Hayley asked.

'We'll go,' she said. 'Who knows, it might improve the day.'

'What do we do until then?' I said.

'I am going to get a drink,' Charlie said. 'I'd like to rest and cool down.'

'Sounds good,' I said. 'I'll join you. I'm too hot to walk around the town. Is anyone else interested?'

'Sure,' Harry said. The girls nodded.

'Thanks again for your help,' I said. 'It's nice to meet you as well. We haven't made any friends until now.'

Charlie smiled. She said something in French to Anthony. Anthony got in the jeep and drove up the street.

Charlie took us to a café next to a tall yellow bar. The bar had a name I couldn't read. We sat outside under a big blue and white umbrella and drank Retsina out of shot glasses. Charlie explained to us that she was from a place called La Ciotat, in the south of France, and that they had come to Greece in a boat as part of their tour. She played the guitar and Anthony was a singer and apparently, in France, they were reasonably famous.

'So what are all your names?' Charlie asked us. 'I have forgotten them already, please forgive me.'

'I'm Will,' I said. 'This is Harry, this is Hayley, and this is Charlotte.'

'You are from England?'

'Yes,' I said. 'We're staying in Liménas on the other side of the island.'

'Are you in the town?' She looked at me.

'No, just outside,' I said.

'That's nice. Is it big?'

'The apartment?'

'Oui.'

'It's quaint. There's a pool and a bar and it's quiet. The staff are really good people.'

'It sounds like a nice place,' Charlie said. 'I'd like to return to Liménas sometime.'

'It's not a big island,' Harry said.

'No, it is not.'

'You're lucky you can afford to rent a car,' Harry said. He sounded a little bitter.

CONVERSATIONS IN JUNE

'Where's your boat?' I asked Charlie.

'It is in the harbour. That's where my brother is now. He is very tired and will sleep for a long time.'

'Can we see your boat?' I asked. I was kicked under the table.

'No. It is too early,' Charlie said. She looked at her watch. 'And I want to go to the beach and bathe. Will you come with me?'

'Sure,' Harry said. 'Are you guys coming?'

The girls shrugged. I nodded. We left the café and walked down to the beach. Charlie removed her dress and waded into the sea.

'Come in!' she called. 'The water is fine.'

I was tired of the tension so I left the girls and joined Charlie in the water. Harry came with me. I offered a cigarette to Charlie.

'Thank you very much,' she said. I lit it for her and tossed my lighter onto the beach. I felt alight now. Somehow being with the French girl made me feel happy. A part of me felt drunk.

When we got out of the water I asked the girls if they were alright.

'We're happy here,' Charlotte said.

'We've been talking about France,' Hayley said. 'And we've been watching you.'

'You have nice friends, Will,' Charlie said.

I got dressed with Harry. There was music coming from the streets now. 'What's that?' I asked.

'That's the music night,' Charlie said. 'It's coming from the yellow bar.'

'Are we going over now?'

'If you like,' Charlie said.

She put her clothes on and we made our way to the bar. Inside there was a band playing on a small stage. They were Greek and they all had big smiles. It was hot. There were fans spinning slowly on the ceiling and every corner of the room was badly lit. The man behind the bar had a large smile and his skin was like leather and he asked us what we would drink. The girls wanted Retsina. I said to hell with it and bought my own bottle. Harry ordered whiskey. 'With lots of ice,' he said, pointing at the counter. We stayed standing because there were no free tables. The band played well and there was cheering and clapping and dancing all round.

Another band came on at seven o'clock and we had more drinks and everyone was talking.

'I prefer this band,' Harry said.

'They're from America,' I said.

'I like their style.'

The band were playing a cover of a lesser known Chuck Berry song, I don't remember which.

'The girls are talking now,' Harry said.

CONVERSATIONS IN JUNE

I glanced at them. 'Good,' I said. 'I was getting sick of the silence. Do you think this Charlie is an honest girl?'

'I don't know. She's good looking though. What are we going to do about getting back?'

'I don't care.' I drank. 'Maybe sleep on the beach. I've never slept on a beach before.'

'What about the French girl's boat?' Harry asked. 'Do you think she'll invite us on?'

I laughed. 'You really want to see her boat don't you?'

'I've always wanted a yacht.'

I smiled. 'It's good to see the girls laughing again,' I said.

'I know what you mean. It's also good to see you smiling.' Harry finished his drink. At last we found a table big enough for us all to sit around.

'Would you like some Retsina?' I asked Harry.

'Go on then,' he said.

I left my seat and went to the bar. I got talking to a potbellied man I didn't know. He asked me where I was from. I told him I was from England. He put his hand on my arm and asked me if I wanted to dance. I said no and he left. Then the barman asked what I wanted. 'Just a wine glass,' I said. He gave it to me right away and I returned to the table. Charlie and the girls were smiling. I sat down.

'Thanks again for bringing my friends here,' I said to Charlie.

'*S'il vous plaît*. It is no problem. Do not say anything about it again. You are very sweet and kind.'

I smiled at her and drank. 'How long does this music go on for tonight?' I said.

'Oh, past midnight.'

'What's there to do afterwards?'

'We can stay in the bar,' Charlie said. 'Or go to the beach for a swim.'

'Sounds alright. We'll have to think about getting back at some point. I don't think anyone here wants to leave it too late.'

I drank a little more and sat back, thinking.

'I have not known you and your friends for long,' Charlie said, 'but you are a nice bunch and you are very kind. I will think about inviting you to my yacht. If the night goes well I will see how I feel.' She looked at me. Her eyes were smiling. I smiled and looked into my drink. 'We should eat something.'

'Do they serve food?' Harry asked.

'Oui. All night.'

'Excellent.'

'We'll eat then,' said Charlotte. 'Do they have a menu?'

'I'll get one,' I said. At the bar I was told that they were only serving fries and olives.

CONVERSATIONS IN JUNE

'We are too busy to cook,' the barman explained. He was sweating badly. 'I am sorry, my friend.'

'It's fine. We'll have fries,' I said. 'For five.'

'I'll get on it,' the barman said, smiling. He clicked his fingers. Our food came an hour later. The fries did not look cooked.

'What the hell is this?' Harry said. He was very drunk now. 'These are awful.' So he ate a bowl of olives instead. 'And I hate these things but it's all we have I suppose.'

'I won't eat olives,' Charlotte said. 'And I'd smoke if I had any cigarettes.'

'Still fresh out?' I said. I checked my pockets.

'It is alright,' Charlie said. 'I have cigarettes.' She took one from out of her bra and handed it to Charlotte. Charlotte took it without question. She was too drunk to care where it had come from.

'That was surprising,' Harry said.

'Pardon?'

'I've never seen a person tuck cigarettes down there before.'

Charlie grinned. 'Oh, well, when you have no pockets it is a good place to put them.'

I felt Hayley give Harry a sharp nudge from under the table.

'Better keep your eyes off her,' I said to him.

At three o'clock the lights went up and the bar emptied.

'What are we going to do now?' Harry asked. 'Looks like the place is closing up.'

Charlotte suggested we go down to the beach.

'Yeah. Let's go roll in the sand,' I said. 'What do you want to do, Charlie?'

'Go to the beach with your friends,' she said, shrugging.

Charlie gave Charlotte another cigarette. I was glad they had made friends. 'Thank you,' Charlotte said.

'And you are all invited to my boat,' Charlie said. 'Oui. I like you all. You have been very good to me.'

'And you've been good to us,' I said. She put her hand on my leg and laughed. She was very drunk and I wished that I was too.

We left the bar and stumbled down to the beach. It was cool and there was a salty breeze coming in off the Aegean. Charlie held my hand and Charlotte was on my arm. Harry collapsed on the sand and spread out like a starfish.

'He's out,' I said, 'and probably will be for the rest of the night.'

'He can watch our things,' Charlotte said.

'Come on,' I said. 'Let's go in the sea.'

CONVERSATIONS IN JUNE

We stripped and charged into the warm dark sea. For half an hour we danced and splashed in the surf. It was exhilarating and I felt happy, but when the laughter came to an end I realised just how lonely I really was, and for the rest of the night I stayed on the beach with Charlie whilst watching the two girls swim. Charlie's head was on my shoulder. I wasn't sure why. She was drunk. Very drunk. And I wasn't in the mood to move her away. It was nice to have company.

'Are you alright?' she asked me.

'I am,' I said.

'You look sad.'

'I always look sad.'

'Don't be sad.'

'I'm not,' I said.

'I don't believe you.'

'I'm alright.'

'Tell me what's wrong with you.' She sat up and faced me. 'Is it them? Is it me? Have I done something to upset you? Am I too forward? Do you not like this?'

'No. It isn't you, or them.'

'What is the matter?'

'Never mind,' I said.

'Are you tired? You want to sleep?'

'I am a little tired, yes. I could sleep.'

She returned to her original position on my shoulder. This time she put her hand on my stomach. I felt the hairs on my arms stand on end.

'You're very drunk,' I said.

'Oui. Oui. I am happy. Drunk and happy.'

I wasn't sure what do to. Part of me wanted this, part of me didn't. We hardly knew each other. And you must understand, she was truly very drunk.

'We'll go back when your friends are tired. We have had a good day.'

'We have,' I said.

'You are a good person, Will. You remind me of a man I met in Rome.'

'What was his name?'

'Jean.'

'That's a good name. Better than Will.'

'You have a nice name.'

I sighed.

'What is the matter?'

'Oh. Just thoughts,' I said.

'Tell me.'

'Maybe later.'

'Okay.' She kissed my shoulder.

'Why are you kissing me?' I asked.

'Do you not like it?' she asked. I wasn't entirely sure what to say. For some reason I felt very stupid for asking her.

CONVERSATIONS IN JUNE

'Are you always this passionate?' I asked.
'Oui.'
'You're terribly nice,' I said.
'So are you.'
'We haven't know each other long,' I said.
'I won't be in Greece forever,' she said. 'To be honest with you, Will, I am quite lonely. I do not get to meet many people. I like you. There is something about you I like very much. You do not mind that? Do you not mind that I have a lot of love and no-one to give it to?'
'No,' I said. 'I don't mind.'
'If you are sure,' she said.
'I'm no different than anyone else,' I said.
'You are quite different.'
'Thanks. But I disagree. I can't see it.'
'I am sorry,' she said.
'What for?'
'For being close like this.'
'I said I don't mind. To hell with minding things. I'm done caring.'

She moved off my shoulder and looked at me. Her face was close to mine. I could tell by the way her eyes looked through me that she was way out of her head. She was extremely handsome under the dim light of the distant streetlamps.

I put my hand on her arm.

'The girls will wonder what we're doing,' I said. 'I could get in trouble. I tend to make people angry when I get involved with girls.'

'You are with the Charlotte girl?' She looked alarmed suddenly.

'No,' I said. 'We're not together.'

'I am sorry.' She moved away. All her warmth left me and I felt lonelier than ever.

'I said we're not together.'

'Okay.'

'We're friends. Harry and Hayley are the ones who are together.'

'They are good people,' Charlie said.

'Yes. They are.'

'You are all good people.'

'So are you,' I said.

'I like you. I like the English. They are nice sometimes. But some of them are pigs.'

'I'm half Italian.'

'That is interesting.' She put her hand on my left cheek. 'You have good structure in your face. And you have nice skin.'

'That's the sun,' I said. 'I don't really have nice skin.'

'You should not be so hard on yourself.'

'Well, I guess not. I'm sorry.'

She ran her fingers over my chest.

CONVERSATIONS IN JUNE

'What are you doing?' I asked. Then she kissed me before I could say anything else. I put my hand on her arm. She kissed me again. The palm of my other hand was pressed into the sand.

Then she put her hand on me.

'Please,' I said. 'Don't.'

'What's wrong?'

'Don't. Not there. Not now.'

'Later?'

'No,' I said. 'Not ever.'

'What is the matter?'

'I can't. I just can't.'

'Why not?' Charlie asked.

'It's just. There's... someone.'

She looked at me carefully. 'I am sorry.'

'It's okay.'

'Where is she? Is she at home?'

'No,' I said.

'Where is she?'

'She went to Canada,' I said. 'But she isn't coming back.'

'Oh. Did she leave you?'

I felt my throat close up. Then I explained to her what had happened.

'I am so sorry, Will.'

She hugged me. I closed my eyes. Something between us disintegrated.

'I am so sorry,' she said again.

'It's alright,' I said.

She kissed me on the cheek and put her hand on my stomach. It was nice on my stomach now. It didn't bother me anymore.

'Thanks for your concern,' I said. 'I'm sorry.'

'You are wonderful,' she said. 'Do not ever be sorry. I can see now that you are hurt.'

'I just can't do it,' I said, feeling like I had disappointed her. 'I know that by now I should be able to... but I haven't been able to ever since.'

'I understand.'

'Thank you,' I said. 'Because I don't think I ever will.'

CONVERSATIONS IN JUNE

OCTOBER 6th

I drove slowly up to the house and parked around the back under the trees. It was cloudy and the air was chilly. There were no lights on in the house. I knocked on the glass of the front door and waited. There was no answer so I went around to the patio and found Robin standing alone in her wedding dress. She was looking into a tall mirror. Her back was to me.

'Robin,' I said.

She turned on her heel.

'Oh. Will. You startled me.'

'What are you doing?' I asked.

'Thinking.'

I didn't ask what she was thinking about. That was obvious enough.

'Are you alright?' I said.

'Yeah. I'm okay.' She smiled. 'I'll be good.'

'Where's Abby?'

'With Jordan,' Robin said.

'I see.'

'Are you alright, Will? You look it. You're tan and your hair is wavy.'

I sat down on a chair.

'Yeah, I'm okay,' I said.

'Did you have a nice time in Greece?'

'It was alright,' I said.

She asked me a few more mundane questions. I answered them all, slowly, as they came out. What was the weather like. Did you take lots of photos. Did you buy anything nice. Did you do anything nice. Was Harry okay. Was Charlotte okay. Was Hayley okay. Did Harry bug Hayley. Did Harry fight with her. Did Charlotte talk about Isaac. Did you meet anyone.

'Yes,' I said.

'A girl?'

'She was French,' I said. 'We spent a few days with her. She's very famous in France.'

'What was her name?' Robin asked.

'Charlie. That's what she called herself anyway. Her real name is Danielle Bedel.'

'I've never heard of her. Was she friendly?'

'She was very nice,' I said. 'Very much the social type. It wasn't the same when she left.'

'Where did she go?'

'She went off down the islands somewhere,' I said. 'I hope to see her again someday.'

I felt sad. I was exhausted with feeling sad.

'Will.'

'Yes?'

'Are you okay?'

'Yes.'

'Are you sure?'

CONVERSATIONS IN JUNE

Robin sat with me. 'Are you still thinking about Sophia?' she asked.

'I've thought about her every day since I lost her,' I said.

'I'm sorry. I really am. But the road goes on.'

What a horrible cliché, I thought. Robin put her arm around me. I wanted to say something – anything to stop me from getting upset.

'What are you dressed like that for?' I asked.

She lowered her head.

'I'm sorry,' I said. 'That was insensitive. I shouldn't have asked.'

'Don't worry. I just thought I'd put it on. I wanted to see what it was like. I wanted to see myself in it. Because now I don't thi –'

'Stop,' I interrupted.

She put her closed hand to her lips and sniffed. She held there for a moment. Then she sighed and rubbed her eyes. I put my arm around her.

'Don't worry,' I said. 'You're better off without Jordan.'

'Do you think so?' she asked.

'I've always thought so to be honest with you.'

'Why did you never say?'

'Because he was yours,' I said. 'I didn't want to throw a spanner in the works. Sorry. That's a terrible cliché. I ought to know better than that.'

'Do you think I should've stayed with him?' Robin asked.

'Absolutely not,' I said. 'He was no good for you anymore. He's become a peevish drunk.'

'Oh Will. Why didn't you tell me?'

'I'm telling you now.'

She smiled. I rubbed her arm. 'Come on,' I said. 'One day you'll be able to wear this dress for real. And everyone will be there for you, and everything will be perfect, and you will finally be happy.'

'I don't think the world works that way,' Robin said.

She put her head in her hands.

'Don't you get like that now,' I said. 'You'll have me going if you start.'

She laughed a little. I held her closer.

'Is it normal for me to miss Abigail this much?'

'Yes,' I said. 'It is.'

'I'm so afraid,' Robin said. There was a change in her voice. It was no longer soft. 'I'm afraid when she's not here. I feel helpless. I worry and I can't relax and then I get like this. God knows what he'll do to her. God knows what'll happen. I'm so afraid, Will.'

'Don't be afraid,' I said. 'Don't worry yourself. She will be alright.'

'Look at me.' She shook her head. 'I'm a

CONVERSATIONS IN JUNE

grown woman and I'm afraid. What kind of a mother is afraid? Look at me in this fucking dress.' She grabbed the white dress and tugged at it. 'Look at me!'

'Don't do that,' I said. 'We're all liable to break at certain points.'

She began to cry. She cried for a long time.

'We all get scared sometimes, Robin,' I said. 'It doesn't mean you're a bad mother.'

'Do you ever get scared, Will?'

'I do,' I said. 'More often than I would like to admit.'

'What are you afraid of?'

'Oh. Many things. But they come and go. I'm always afraid of losing you, though.'

'Oh Will. Please don't say things like that.'

I swallowed and my eyes glazed over.

'You won't ever lose me,' Robin said. She looked into my eyes. For a couple of minutes we didn't speak.

'When will Abigail be back?' I asked.

'He's dropping her here at three o'clock.'

'Everything will be fine,' I said. 'You'll see.'

'Please stay with me, Will.'

I smiled. 'I was never going to leave you.'

'Please don't ever go. I've been so lonely these past few nights. Nothing helps it anymore.'

'I'll stay for as long as you want.'

'Thank you.'

'It's okay,' I said. Robin smiled. Her cheeks were bright red.

'You know I love you,' I said.

'I love you too,' Robin said.

'I'd be nowhere without you.'

'I know. And I'd be nowhere without you.'

'You make it all bearable,' I said.

'What do I make bearable, Will?'

I looked across the garden. The sun was breaking through the silver clouds. There was colour in the world again.

'Life,' I said. 'And being alone.'

'You are not alone,' Robin said.

'I know. Because I've got you.'

My sister closed her eyes. She was smiling. 'And you've got me.'